Sam was at Gran's house when the wind started to blow.

Rain lashed down.

4

This item should be returned on or before the last date stamped above. If not in demand it may be renewed for a further period by personal application, by telephone, or in writing. The author, title, above number and date due back should be quoted.

W

FRANKLIN WATTS
LONDON • SYDNEY

First published in 2009 by
Franklin Watts
338 Euston Road
London
NW1 3BH

Franklin Watts Australia
Level 17/207 Kent Street
Sydney
NSW 2000

A CIP catalogue record for this book is available
from the British Library.

ISBN 978 0 7496 8515 7 (hbk)
ISBN 978 0 7496 8521 8 (pbk)

Series Editor: Jackie Hamley
Editor: Melanie Palmer
Series Advisor: Dr Hilary Minns
Series Designer: Peter Scoulding

Printed in China

Franklin Watts is a division of
Hachette Children's Books,
an Hachette UK company.
www.hachette.co.uk

Thunder crashed.

"Why?" asked Sam.
"You'll see," said Gran.

She clapped her hands
with the thunder.

So Sam whooshed
with the wind ...

… and leapt with the lightning.

Then it went quiet.
The storm had ended.

"That *was* magical," said Sam.

"There's more magic to come," said Gran.

20

Puzzle Time!

Put these pictures in the right order and retell the story!

excited

cheerful

wise

curious

Which words describe Sam
and which describe Gran?

Turn over for answers!

Notes for adults

TADPOLES are structured to provide support for newly independent readers. The stories may also be used by adults for sharing with young children.

Starting to read alone can be daunting. **TADPOLES** help by providing visual support and repeating words and phrases. These books will both develop confidence and encourage reading and rereading for pleasure.

If you are reading this book with a child, here are a few suggestions:

1. Make reading fun! Choose a time to read when you and the child are relaxed and have time to share the story.
2. Talk about the story before you start reading. Look at the cover and the blurb. What might the story be about? Why might the child like it?
3. Encourage the child to retell the story, using the jumbled picture puzzle as a starting point. Extend vocabulary with the matching words to characters puzzle.
4. Discuss the story and see if the child can relate it to their own experience.
5. Give praise! Remember that small mistakes need not always be corrected.

Answers

Here is the correct order!

1.f 2.a 3.d 4.c 5.e 6. b

Words to describe Sam:
curious, excited

Words to describe Gran:
cheerful, wise